KRYPTO THE SUPERDOG™

Here Comes Krypto

JESSE LEON MCCANN.................................WRITER
MIN S. KU...PENCILLER
JEFF ALBRECHT....................................... INKER
DAVE TANGUAY ....COLOURIST
DAVE TANGUAY .... LETTERER

KRYPTO
The SUPERDOG

SUPERMAN CREATED BY
JERRY SIEGEL AND JOE SHUSTER
BY SPECIAL ARRANGEMENT WITH
THE JERRY SIEGEL FAMILY

Raintree is an imprint of Capstone Global
Library Limited, a company incorporated
in England and Wales having its registered
office at 7 Pilgrim Street, London, EC4V
6LB – Registered company number: 6695582

First published by Raintree in 2014
The moral rights of the proprietor have
been asserted.

Originally published by DC Comics in the
US in single magazine form as Krypto The
Superdog #1.

Ashley C. Andersen Zantop Publisher
Michael Dahl Editorial Director
Donald Lemke & Sean Tulien Editors
Bob Lentz Art Director
Hilary Wacholz Designer

DC COMICS
Kristy Quinn Original US Editor

ISBN 978 1 406 27950 4

Printed in China by Nordica.
0314/CA21400432
17 16 15 14
10 9 8 7 6 5 4 3 2

British Library Cataloguing in Publication
Data
A full catalogue record for this book is
available from the British Library.

I WISH I HAD *THE WORDS* TO DESCRIBE THE *GREATEST DOG* OF ALL ...

KRYPTO
THE *SUPERDOG*

KRYPTO WAS JUST A *PUPPY* WHEN HE LEFT HIS HOME PLANET, *KRYPTON.*

FWHOOOM!

KRYPTO WASN'T *TOO SCARED*, BECAUSE HE KNEW HE WOULD ONLY BE GONE FOR *ONE DAY.*

THEN HE WOULD RETURN TO HIS *BEST FRIEND*, A LITTLE BOY NAMED *KAL-EL.*

BUT SOMETHING *WENT WRONG,* AND KRYPTO'S SHIP CHANGED COURSE.

ZZZT! CRACKLE!

WARNING! WARNING! PLANETARY EVACUATION SEQUENCE ACTIVATED!

COORDINATES SET FOR **EARTH.**

HIBERNATION GAS RELEASED.

PSSSSSSS

SLEEP TIGHT!

THAT WAS THE *LAST* KRYPTO SAW OF KRYPTON'S SUN. HE WAS HEADING FOR A NEW *SOLAR SYSTEM*—AND A *NEW WORLD!*

AND, AFTER *MANY, MANY* YEARS, HE ARRIVED!

OPEN **SLEEPING POD** TO AWAKEN PASSENGER.

BOY, DID I *OVERSLEEP!* I'M ALMOST GROWN UP!

APPROACHING **EARTH.** PREPARE FOR LANDING.

COLLAR ... IDENTIFICATION TAG.

HUH?

TOUCHDOWN IN **TEN** SECONDS. PLEASE **RETURN** TO YOUR SEAT.

FWOOOSH!!

CRYPTO'S SHIP LANDED, AND HE GOT HIS FIRST *UP-CLOSE* LOOK AT EARTH ...

IT'S SO *BEAUTIFUL* AND *GREEN* HERE! AND THE SUN'S SO YELLOW!

BUT, I'M *ALL ALONE.* I COULD USE A *BEST FRIEND* —A *BOY,* JUST LIKE KAL-EL!

¡ONNNNNK! ¡ONNNNNK!

YIPE! I DON'T REMEMBER *THAT* BACK HOME!

I DON'T REMEMBER *JUMPING* THIS HIGH, EITHER!

HEY, WAIT A MINUTE! I'M *FLYING!*

LOOK, GERTIE, THEY'VE *LEARNED* HOW TO FLY!

WHOOSH!

WE'RE *IN TROUBLE* NOW!

A *CITY!* THIS LOOKS LIKE THE *PERFECT* PLACE TO FIND A BOY!

WELCOME TO METROPOLIS

AND FIND A BOY HE DID!

HI, GUYS, I'M *KEVIN.* ANYBODY WANT TO TOSS A FEW?

SURE! GO *WAY* OUT, AND I'LL THROW YOU A *LONG ONE.*

THEY EVEN *BUILT THINGS* TOGETHER!

WHACK!
WHACK!
WHACK!

A SHORT TIME LATER, KRYPTO FETCHED HIS *ROCKET* FROM THE FOREST....

....AND *BURIED IT* IN THE BACK YARD. IT BECAME THEIR *SECRET HEADQUARTERS!*

KRYPTO

THESE ARE THE *PICTURES* MY KRYPTON BOY DREW.

WHOA! ALIEN ART!

MAN, THIS IS *SO COOL!* I CAN EVEN WATCH *CARTOONS!*

THIS IS THE METRO NEWS 'COPTER! T[] SITUATION HAS BEC[] *DESPERATE!* THER[] BEEN AN *ENGIN[] EXPLOSION* ON T[] SHIP, MILES OUTS[] METROPOLIS HARB[] IT *CAN'T MOVE* AND TAKING ON WATE[]

CH-CLICK!

LIVE

... TO MAKE MATTERS *WORSE*, THE SHIP IS FILLED WITH *ZOO ANIMALS!* SUPERMAN IS NOT EXPECTED BACK FROM HIS *SPACE MISSION* UNTIL THIS AFTERNOON, AND WITHOUT THE MAN OF STEEL, THE SITUATION *LOOKS HOPELESS!*

METRO

KRYPTO KNEW IT WAS UP TO *HIM* TO *SAVE THE DAY!* BUT HE NEEDED A *DISGUISE*, AND KEVIN THOUGHT HE HAD THE *PERFECT* ONE ...

THE END

METROPOLIS, THE NEXT AFTERNOON ...

AH, WHAT A *BEAUTIFUL* DAY!

YOU SAID IT, K-DOG! *PERFECT* WEATHER FOR A *PICNIC!*

HEY, KEVIN, HOW ABOUT *WHIPPING UP* SOME HAMBURGERS, FRIES AND MILKSHAKES? OH! AND A *SIDE ORDER* OF GRILLED SALMON, POTATO SALAD, FRIED CHICKEN, CORN ON THE...

ZEET ZEET ZEET ZEET ZEET!

IT'S THE ROCKET'S *EMERGENCY MONITOR!* SOMEONE *NEEDS* OUR HELP!

SIGH! A HERO'S WORK IS *NEVER* DONE!

ACE? AT'S UP?

I COULD USE YOUR... *ASSISTANCE.* BATMAN IS OUT OF THE COUNTRY, AND...A *SITUATION* HAS DEVELOPED IN *GOTHAM CITY.*

IT STARTED THIS MORNING ... EARTHQUAKES, BUT UNLIKE ANY I'VE EVER SEEN. THEY STARTED *SMALL*, BUT THEY'VE BEEN GETTING *BIGGER* AND *BIGGER*...AFFECTING A WIDER AREA. AND THAT'S NOT ALL... THE EARTHQUAKES HAPPEN EVERY FIFTEEN MINUTES...ON THE DOT.

RRRRRUMBLE!

RRRRRUMBLE!

I HAVE A *THEORY* ABOUT WHAT'S HAPPENING... BUT *NO TIME* TO GO INTO THAT NOW. MEET ME AT *GOTHAM HARBOR*, BEHIND THE OLD *ACME INDUSTRIES* WAREHOUSE, AS SOON AS YOU CAN...

POK!

...OW.

I GOT IT!

WOW! *THANKS,* SUPERDOG! THAT WAS THE *BIGGEST EARTHQUAKE* YET!

YOU HAVE THOSE *EVERY* FIFTEEN MINUTES? SHEESH! I DUNNO IF I CAN *TAKE* IT!

THAT'S MY *DAD!* GOODBYE, SUPERDOG! I HOPE YOU CAN *SAVE* THE CITY!

Honk! Honk!

WOOF! RUFF! WOOF! (WE'LL TRY OUR BEST, SEAN!)

MINUTES LATER, AT THE 55TH STREET SUBWAY STATION ...

HMM ... I DON'T SEE *BATHOUND* ANYWHERE.

WAIT! THERE'S SOMEONE I DO *RECOGNIZE!*

IMMY E RAT! NOW YOU SOMETHING DO WITH THIS!

NOW HERE'S *AN INTERROGATION* I COULD REALLY *SINK MY TEETH* INTO!

H-AH-AH! A, SUPES! STREAKY!

L-LOOK, IT WASN'T *MY FAULT!* THE JOKER'S HYENAS *MADE* ME DO IT! HOW WAS I TO KNOW THEY'D WANNA *BRING GOTHAM DOWN* AROUND OUR EARS?!

KEEP TALKING.

THE JOKER DEVELOPED A NEW *LAUGHING GAS* THAT'S *TIME-RELEASED* TO MAKE YA LAUGH EVERY *FIFTEEN MINUTES.* BUD AND LOU MADE ME SHOW THEM WHERE *EVERY RATS' NEST* IS UNDER THE CITY.

DID YOU KNOW THERE'S *TWO RATS FOR EVERY PERSON* IN GOTHAM CITY DOWN HERE? THE HYENAS PLAN TO *GAS EVERY ONE* OF THEM!

FIFTEEN MINUTES? WHY DOES THAT SOUND SO *FAMILIAR?*

"EVERY FIFTEEN MINUTES, THEY ALL START *LAUGHING* AND *GIGGLING!* THAT'S WHEN THE *TROUBLE* STARTS!"

HEE HEE HEE HEE HEE HEE!

SHAKE! RATTLE! ROLL!

RRRRRRUMBLE!

OH! *MILLIONS* OF RATS A-SHAKIN' AND A-QUAKIN' AT THE *SAME TIME* AND THE *EARTH MOVES!* AND THE QUAKES ARE GETTING STRONGER BECAUSE THE HYENAS ARE GASSING MORE AND MORE RATS!

NOT TO MENTION ALL THE OTHER *ASSORTED ANIMALS* THAT LIVE DOWN THERE! MICE, RACCOONS, POSSUMS, GOPHERS, MOLES ...

OKAY, WE GET THE PICTURE!

RRRRRRUMBLE!

KRACKK-A-RRRRUMBLE!

SUPERDOG, THE CEILING!

I SEE IT! COME ON, STREAKY!

EEEEEEEK!

HEY! WHEN I'M *DISTRACTED* BY HELPING PEOPLE, I DON'T GET THE *JELLY* FEELING IN MY *BELLY!*

ZZZZIP!

THAT'S *GOOD,* STREAKY!

SEVERAL MINUTES LATER ...

LET'S GO!

FOUND THEM—THE JOKER'S HYENAS! AND IT LOOKS LIKE BATHOUND'S *TAKING THEM ON* ALONE!

NOW THAT GOTHAM CITY IS *SHAKING* IN ITS *BOOTIES*, EVERYTHING IS *OURS* FOR THE TAKING! HEH HEH HEH HEH!

WHAT SHOULD WE *LOOT FIRST*, LOU?

HOW 'BOUT THE *FIRST* NATIONAL BANK, BUD?! HAH HAH HAH HAH HAH!

YOU WON'T BE MAKING ANY *WITHDRAWALS* TODAY!

OH LOOK, LOU! IT'S THE *CAPED CLOWNS!* HEH HEH!

WE HATE TO BE *RUDE*, SUPES, BUT IT'S *TIME* FOR ANOTHER *ESCAPE*, IN 3... 2... 1...

WHAT THE *HEE-HAW*?!

THERE AIN'T *NO SHAKIN'*, LOU! MAYBE WE SHOULD *HOTFOOT* IT OUTTA HERE!

SORRY ABOUT THAT, FELLAS. BUT A *FRIEND* DEVELOPED THE *ANTIDOTE* TO YOUR LAUGHING GAS!

THERE'LL BE *NO MORE* EARTHQUAKES!

A FRIEND WITH AN ANTIDOTE? WHAT FRIEND?

THAT WOULD BE *ME*.

AFTER YOU *GASSED* ME... I COULDN'T *MOVE*. LUCKILY, STREAKY *FETCHED* THE ANTIDOTE FROM MY *UTILITY BELT* AND CURED ME...OF THAT *INCESSANT* LAUGHTER.

AND THANKS TO THEIR *SUPER-SPEED*... SUPERDOG AND STREAKY *QUICKLY* CURED ALL THE *RATS*, TOO.

OUTSIDE ...

THANKS FOR THE HELP, CHUMS... *I'LL* TAKE IT FROM HERE!

THERE'S *ONE LAST* THING I WANT TO DO WITH THESE GUYS.

WHOOOSH!

AW! I WANTED TO HAVE THE *LAST* LAUGH, LOU!

Superdog Jokes!

WHAT KIND OF DOG TELLS THE TIME?

A WATCH DOG!

WHAT DO YOU CALL A SUPERDOG
WEARING METAL ARMOUR?

KRYPTO-KNIGHT!

WHY IS A TREE LIKE A BIG DOG?

THEY BOTH HAVE A LOT OF BARK!

WHAT DO YOU CALL A
DOG THAT MUMBLES?

A MUTT-ERER!

Creators

JESSE LEON MCCANN WRITER

Jesse Leon McCann is a *New York Times* Top-Ten Children's Book Writer, as well as a prolific all-ages comics writer. His credits include Pinky and the Brain, Animaniacs, and Looney Tunes for DC Comics; Scooby-Doo and Shrek 2 for Scholastic; and The Simpsons and Futurama for Bongo Comics. He lives in Los Angeles with his wife and four cats.

MIN SUNG KU PENCILLER

As a young child, Min Sung Ku dreamt of becoming a comic book illustrator. At six years old, he drew a picture of Superman standing behind the American flag. He has since achieved his childhood dream, having illustrated popular licensed comics properties such as the Justice League, Batman Beyond, Spider-Man, Ben 10, Phineas & Ferb, the Replacements, the Proud Family, Krypto the Superdog, and, of course, Superman. Min lives with his lovely wife and their beautiful twin daughters, Elisia and Eliana.

DAVE TANGUAY COLOURIST/LETTERER

David Tanguay has over 20 years of experience in the comic book industry. He has worked as an editor, layout artist, colourist, and letterer. He has also done web design, and he taught computer graphics at the State University of New York.

Glossary

GOTHAM CITY Batman and Ace the Bathound's home city

INTERROGATION questioning someone in detail, often in order to determine if he or she is guilty or innocent of a crime

KRYPTON Superman and Krypto the Superdog's home planet

METROPOLIS Superman and Krypto the Superdog's adopted home city

MISDEEDS immoral or evil acts

RECOGNIZE to see someone and know who the person is, or to understand a situation and know it is true or right

UTILITY BELT Batman and Ace the Bathound both wear Utility Belts that hold all sorts of tools and crime-fighting gadgets

Visual Questions & Prompts

1. WHAT DO YOU THINK THIS OBJECT IS THAT KRYPTO GAVE KEVIN WHEN THEY FIRST MET?

2. WHY DO YOU THINK KRYPTO'S SHIP'S COMPUTER MADE HIM FALL INTO A DEEP SLEEP WHILE HE TRAVELLED?

3. WHAT IS HAPPENING IN THIS PANEL? WHAT DOES KRYPTO SEE, AND HOW?

HEY, THE HYENAS *ESCAPED*! OOOH! I'M GONNA GIVE THEM *SUCH* A SCRATCH!

WAIT! *WHAT'S THAT* I HEAR?

OH, NO!

THE *RAILS* WERE *DAMAGED* BY THE QUAKES...CAN'T STOP!

SCRAAAAAH

3

4. WHY DON'T SUPERCAT AND SUPERDOG WANT CHOCOLATE MILKSHAKES AT THE END OF THIS BOOK WHEN KEVIN OFFERS TO MAKE SOME?

NO, THANK YOU!

WHY? WHAT'S WRONG?

SORRY, KEVIN. IT'S TOTALLY THE *WRONG TIME* TO OFFER US A COUPLE OF *SHAKES*!

KRYPTO

4

Raintree